CHRONICLES OF THE DRAGONMASTERS

KATIE CROSS

KCW

CONTENTS

Chronicles of the Dragonmasters

YA Fantasy

Published by KC Writing. Visit www.katiecrossbooks.com for more information about the author, updates, or new books.

CHAPTER 1

PARKER

irst Month of Fall

I am Parker, High Dragonmaster.

So begins a new book recording the dealings of the Dragonmasters.

The leaves transform into an awning of sunburst colors overhead, like a patchwork quilt in the canopy of Letum Wood. The air is crisp. The gentle turn of summer into fall has always been my favorite time. The most reflective one, at any rate. I enjoy looking over my year. Something about the smell of pumpkin and the taste of fresh leto nuts makes me want to sink into the forest. Today, however, something even greater has filled me with joy.

My son Alfrid's dragon hatched her first egg three days ago.

A beautiful female. Her scales are oddly black; they have not sprouted color. Odd for a hatchling. They normally show hints at least. I've seen this when dragons hatch early, so my concern is not strong. Still, there is fire in her. Riddlis hasn't named her. He forgets, though Alfrid is impatient. I remind

Alfrid that Riddlis is 180 years old. One simply doesn't make demands of the brood sire.

With such age comes a much slower mind, I have noticed. It pains me. Riddlis has wild ideas that have begun to stir fear in my heart. Ideas like complete brood isolation. Utter disregard for witches outside the Dragonmaster village. Never speaking with the other dragon races. How could we? Although he will not admit it, Riddlis rarely speaks with Deasylva. She has requested help with specific tasks. He has ignored her.

I do not enjoy working behind my dragon's back.

Another thing has transpired—not so joyful. Sarai, the third daughter of the headstrong Dragonmaster Mikal Spence, was paired with Talis. Riddlis insisted.

I have my concerns. Talis is young, barely into adolescence at eighteen. He is much quieter than most dragons. More prone to annoyance with hints of a greater temper. His fire burns hot, bright, and fast. I fear we cannot control him, nor that Riddlis will try. Talis needs a rider who will connect with him, not dominate him.

Sarai, like her older sister Celeste, will do nothing of the sort.

Sarai is intelligent and extremely confident for only fifteen years old. Motivated. Straightforward. Difficult to speak with. Just like all the Spence girls, except for Tea, who has a hint of compassion and mischief. Then, I suppose when a mam dies in childbirth and leaves six girls and a husband, what else would result? One could never call the family warm, though Sarai is not glacial. Still, Riddlis is the brood sire. I, the High Dragonmaster. He rules the dragons, and I rule the witches. My concerns fall on deaf ears.

Perhaps the two of them will surprise me.

A disease has broken out amongst the dragons in the western section of Letum Wood. Riddlis and I flew there a week ago. An odd issue. In all the *Chronicles* volumes before mine, I've never read a report of a dragon with a drippy nose. These are sneezing bucketful of mucus. Celeste and Perris are flying to the Western Network broods on my request. They will inquire after potions to help. None of the dragons have lost their heat, yet I worry.

The forest fares well.

I am Parker, High Dragonmaster.

First Month of Winter

The cold settles into my bones with a frosty breath.

Even Deasylva seems to retreat into the heart of the Ancients, where their sap pulses sluggishly. Letum Wood holds on to the bitter air with jealous arms. Still, I cannot stand to be inside. Both Alfrid and I find reasons to be with the dragons, who sometimes share their warmth. Riddlis prefers his warm cave and long, luxurious naps. I hear the dragons' surly thoughts constantly. It bothers me, but after twelve years as High Dragonmaster, I've learned to live with them.

Riddlis refuses to name the new hatchling, who finally shows signs of color. Burgundy, I believe, though the veins are faint. She is full of spunk and has bonded with Alfrid and her mam.

A troll has been closing in, attempting to extend its boundaries. Riddlis and I have assigned Stillman and Terris to monitor it every morning. The matadors continue to fly overhead and spray our homes with their tacky scent.

Sarai and Talis have not spoken yet. For my part, I feel it is for the best that they mourn the loss of a more advantageous pairing.

A bouncing, fat baby has been welcomed into the Dragonmaster fold. Nina. A beautiful girl with blue eyes. She is the daughter of Blaine and Caterina, the tenth of her family. Given the planned course of our family tree, Marta and Alfrid will handfast when he is twenty-two and she twenty. That is only a few years from now.

I am Parker, High Dragonmaster.

❲

First Month of Spring

Riddlis has finally named the burgundy hatchling.

Luna.

It means *bright one*. She is intelligent. Sharp. Full of courage—perhaps too much. Alfrid will have his hands full with her.

Riddlis seems to have woken up with the spring. We flew, safely, for an hour last week. Soon, flying will not be safe. His giant heart may fail while we are merged and kill both of us.

No hatchlings have been born.

Talis has finally approached Sarai to begin the merging process. Their lack of trust is painfully clear. Sarai does not understand his low moods. He does not trust her natural drive to prove herself a worthy Dragonmaster. Talis craves affection; he is too needy by half. It seems Sarai cannot give it to him. Her own personality seems to keep her from bonding with him. Perhaps it will be good for them to learn the needs of the other. In this the greatest Dragonmasters and dragons have found their destiny.

The forest has now grown to the edge of the healthy land. The sheer power of Letum Wood astounds me. Deasylva's dominion could stretch over all the land if not prevented by the others of her kind.

The forest fares well.

I am Parker, High Dragonmaster.

FIRST MONTH of Summer

Sultry days have put the dragons in gleeful moods. To us, the heat is unbearable, so thick I feel as if I'm swimming.

We celebrate a bounteous harvest. We have plenty of falla melons, wild berries, and leto nuts to store for winter. Celeste and Perris led the way in battling an out-of-control forest fire last week. Celeste used spells to assist while Perris burned ahead of the blaze to remove the fuel. This was beneficial because Talis and Sarai flew together for the first time since they merged a month ago. Talis fared well—strong flight, quick responses, hot flames. Sarai, however, pushed him beyond what she should have. She is too eager to please her father, who flew with Atris.

Riddlis will not interfere. His current sleep has lasted three days. I fear he may never wake up. I have not heard from Deasylva, though I have met at our rendezvous point twice this season. No further news from the High Priestess, so our annual meeting will not occur this year.

The forest fares well.

I am Parker, High Dragonmaster.

FIRST MONTH of Fall

Talis had the unfortunate luck to find a cohereo tree.

Shelby, the High Dragonmaster before me, swore they'd

removed all of them. Apparently not. Sarai was livid. As his Dragonmaster, she had to pinch the tree's tentacles to free him for almost nine hours. It was a particularly ... *motivated* tree. I hoped such an experience would bring them together, so I left Sarai to it. The tree started to reattach vines she had already pinched, and Sarai tired just shy of nine hours. Utterly frustrated, she left him there all night—unbeknownst to anyone. Talis never alerted me to her abandonment.

By morning, Talis was nearly engulfed by vines. I found out, called her father, and the three of us barely freed him in time. Talis almost died. Once we finished, Talis left without a word. Mikal bore Sarai away by the ear.

I fear for them. In my twelve years as High Dragonmaster, I have never had a pairing fail. Perhaps I should have spoken up sooner, but how could I have? Riddlis declared it, and who can stop the brood sire? Still, there is nothing I can do now.

Pairs patrolling the eastern forest have noticed strange things in the Eastern Network. Frequent fires. Constant emissaries. Bright bursts of magic. They have not been able to explain it. Rumors of war circulate in the villages. I have sent word to the High Priestess.

Luna is a yearling and has already communicated with me on purpose. Hatchlings often send thoughts to me on accident during the first five years of life. For Luna, it has been no accident. She speaks of her mam. Of Alfrid. Of the trees. She even spoke of Deasylva. Why should I be surprised? Just because the goddess doesn't speak with me of late, why not the dragons?

The forest fares well.

I am Parker, High Dragonmaster.

～

First Month of Winter

Winter has set in with a brutal chill. As I write, my ink freezes. I keep it warm in one hand while the wind howls outside.

A new handfasting has taken place.

Samuel, an apothecary who wandered into the circle and stayed after he met my eldest daughter, Rachael, has given a cord of engagement to her. This is rather uncomfortable for me and for all the families.

Nearly all our matches are decided by necessity, not romance. Whimsical love means nothing compared to surviving Letum Wood or rearing children to merge with dragons. No outsider could understand. Diluting the Dragonmaster blood has always made many nervous. Of course, it has been diluted many times out of necessity. We cannot interbreed the way forest dragons do. But it has been done carefully, with great attention to those brought in. Samuel has lived amongst us but shows no inclination toward the dragons. A major concern. Still, the Parker family line is strong. It has survived since the Mortal Wars.

I have allowed this handfasting. For my leniency, Rachael has Talis and Sarai to thank. Forcing a witch to care for a dragon wouldn't serve anyone.

I spoke with Sarai last week and addressed Talis's recent withdrawal symptoms. She seemed surprised and hadn't noticed. I could see her resentment. I imagine that I know her thoughts. *A good dragon shouldn't require coddling.* I tried to speak with Talis, but he sulked away.

This has been my greatest fear.

We head into winter with many supplies after a successful trade run last season, though we have many traps to fix and lines to set. The hatchlings continue to grow. Seven wreaths made of vines and bright white flowers descended from the Ancients at our latest monthly gathering. I can only presume that Deasylva is pleased. I go to bed. The night is late, quiet, and sweet.

The forest fares well.

I am Parker, High Dragonmaster.

CHAPTER 2
CELESTE

Third Month of Winter

I am Celeste, High Dragonmaster.

We lost our oldest brood sire and Dragonmaster. Two weeks ago, Riddlis returned to Halla, the land from which all dragons come and eventually return. No doubt he has gained his reward. Parker has been burned on the pyre according to our custom. Letum Wood has already accepted her servants back into her soil.

There was much speculation about their deaths, but I silenced the rumors. Both Parker and Riddlis died mid-flight two weeks ago. I blame Parker. For a Dragonmaster of his experience, he should have known better than to fly with a dragon so old. Still, I give honor to Parker and all he did. In a society blessed with long life, he was not a young man at eighty-four, but he had many years left.

I ascend his place by common vote of witch and dragon. Deasylva approved—which surprised me. I am only thirty-eight and not yet handfasted. She spoke with me shortly after the vote was cast. To the specifics of our personal communication, I will not refer. Suffice it to say that Deasylva has overridden votes in the past. I believe her approval of me stems from my devotion to the dragons and our traditions. I am confident. I excel in flying, magic, and communication.

Perris is my dragon and will tolerate no lax dragons or discipline. Troublemakers like Talis, who shows all the right traits but the wrong training, will be shaped into true dragon leaders. Not even the quiet, uncertain emerald dragon Stellis can escape Perris's sharp eye. I look forward to seeing Perris's poise and power unfold as brood mam.

Speaking of Talis, I have read Parker's entries and agree with his assessment. Few wouldn't. Sarai and Talis are not a good match. Parker should have spoken up. What is the point of our relationship with dragons if not to rule together? I digress from the informational purpose of this narrative. If Talis continues to fly according to Sarai's expectations, and she speaks with him every day, they will maintain a functional relationship. I doubt they will ever be close, which is acceptable. I will not coddle anyone—certainly not Sarai.

Although I'm loath to write about personal matters, I will follow the traditions of my forebears and speak to my transition to High Dragonmaster. The dragons voices in my head are unnerving. Overwhelming. I don't like chaos. They talk at unexpected times, and I feel there is no escape. For the next month, I plan to dedicate my free time to deciphering how to control this communication and the headaches that follow.

I am Celeste, High Dragonmaster.

～

First Month of Fall

There isn't time for luxuries like writing. I will update the most important matters that pertain to the brood when I see fit.

A disease has spread amongst the hatchlings. Their bones don't harden, or perhaps they loosen, as if they're made of jelly. Of ten hatchlings, only three are able to fly. The other seven's wings collapse when they attempt flight. Only Luna seems completely unaffected. Intelligent for such a little thing. She doesn't speak with me yet, but I see her eye me often. She appears to care for Alfrid.

Mitty, our dragon apothecary, works on this hatchling issue.

We desperately need more cotton and linen for textiles, flour through the winter, and tools and traps for hunting. Local villages have become strict in their trade requirements.

In light of this, self-sufficiency seems safest for the families and the brood. Trade is unstable. So are the Network and outside villages. I would ask Deasylva, but it concerns only witches. I have not involved her but have encouraged our witches not assigned to dragons to educate themselves and serve the families with other skills. This has been well received. Two of our witches left last fall, Tayler to become a blacksmith and Markus to start a farm to grow cotton and an assortment of wheat.

Aside from two rider injuries, a dragon that hasn't stopped sneezing for ten days, and increasing belua counts, I was handfasted to Tor Chandler in the spring. An advantageous marriage that will maintain pure bloodlines.

Talis and Sarai continue to interact as little as possible. I'll accept this. It is much like myself and Deasylva. We speak little, and I feel this is best.

The forest and village fare well.

To follow up on my previous entry, I feel it worthy to note that careful meditation, breathing, and thought control have brought the dragon voices under my command. I've learned to block them at will in order to free my thoughts to engage in logical problem-solving.

I am Celeste, High Dragonmaster.

FIRST DAY of Fall

Nothing of significance to note. Yerris has passed to the forests of Halla, an unmarked but content dragon. Her quiet ways have been missed.

Ten more hatchlings were born this past year, bringing our total to fifty. Last year's hatchlings have mostly recovered from the disease. Only two were lost. Some have residual weakness, but their mams hunt for them without issue. I do not fear our numbers are too great yet. Not with all of Letum Wood to roam and hunt.

Luna continues to exceed the others and spoke with me to request a flight not approved for hatchlings. I approved. She was gone three hours but returned with a belua carcass she must have killed on her own. She gave it to the weakened hatchlings without gloating or demands for attention. Perris could hardly reproach her for the long flight. Neither could I. She slept all night afterward.

Met with the High Priestess for an hour in the village of Pember. The Network seems to continue in a stable way, although I have not left the forest to know. The dragons show no inclination toward the castle, which is a good enough sign that our obligation isn't required now. The High Priestess was a quiet little thing, but kind.

Sarai threatened to saddle Talis if he didn't explicitly obey her directions while flying. I agreed with her. No Dragonmaster can afford a wild, untrustworthy dragon. He shot fire at us, burning a tree behind me. Perris leapt onto his back and brought him to the ground in a terrifying display of strength. Talis has put up no other resistance since and speaks to no one. If I were to allow such a thing? Chaos would reign. I loathe nothing more than chaos.

The forest fares well.

I am Celeste, High Dragonmaster.

First Day of Fall

Torrential rains in early summer wiped out the leto nuts, on which we heavily depend in the winter. Ten chickens were killed by passing predators—we did not see them. Most suspect lions, but I believe it's something smaller. The chickens didn't make a sound. Letum Wood conceals many dangers. This winter may be one of them.

Sarai has been spotted with another dragon, Hubris, several times now. Dragonmasters and dragons live and work together—this is accepted. But Sarai has been spending far *too* much time with Hubris, who is strict and severe and opinionated. Unlike Talis. Sarai's wild inclinations and erratic decisions will send Daid to his grave. Not even Talis can hide his jealousy. Perris has no idea how to approach this problem. I have spoken sharply with Sarai. If I need to, I will speak with Talis, who sulks entirely too much.

Fire has broken out (not at our instigation) in ten spots this year. Some of it was clearly set by witches along the Eastern border. I have informed the High Priestess, who has not written back.

Luna continues to grow in intelligence; I am somewhat hopeful that my own child will one day bond with her. This is, I know, the wish of all mams right now. Alfrid seems to have her sole allegiance.

I am with child now, and so is Perris. It is early yet for me; I believe only three months. Perris will lay her egg (or eggs) soon. We planned this accordingly so she can care for her hatchings while I care for my child. Already I search for my temporary replacement but find none acceptable.

The forest fares well.

I am Celeste, High Dragonmaster.

CHAPTER 3
MARI

First Month of Spring

I am Mari ... High Dragonmaster?

How odd it seems!

Celeste is caring for her brand-new child, as any mother should. Maximus, they named him. The baby has a set of lungs I haven't heard the like of in ninety-seven years of life. And I had eleven children! Mark my words, that one will be a Dragonmaster leader or a total madman.

Perris is caring for her young hatchlings at the same time. She had three eggs—beautiful marbling and translucency—but, tragically, only two have survived. The third never hatched and eventually cracked. Saddest day of the year. I wept for poor Perris. Celeste showed up to the burning looking like a mess. Don't you know it—that baby cried the whole time we burned the dead hatchling.

I suppose I should explain how I, of all witches, was appointed High Dragonmaster. No one was more surprised than I, I think. Well ... perhaps Celeste, whenever she found out. Glad I wasn't there for that! Anyway, it was a very odd event. Confusion abounded when Celeste began to have her child a full month early. Luckily, Samuel and Rachael had returned for an unexpected visit, and Samuel guided the birth. A very talented apothecary, that one! He's handy to have around. Handsome, too.

I digress.

The decision of who would guide the brood while Celeste recovered for the traditional two months had not been made before she went into labor and nearly died. Voting was sporadic. Eventually, it narrowed to Marcus or myself, based solely on our age. I've never even merged with a dragon. (When you have eleven children and a perfectly competent Dragonmaster husband, you don't need a giant lizard to care for on top of everything else.)

Anyway, Marcus is only seventy-five but has even less experience with dragons than myself. He always left that to his wife, Daphne, who is far more skilled than he. I admit that I was curious about having all the dragons' voices in my head, so I accepted.

Although I approach the older age of ninety-seven (I am not old! Many of my ancestors lived to 129.), I am still strong. I have never thought to question the way Deasylva runs her forest—living underneath its boughs has been pleasure enough for me—but I am grateful for this chance. Never thought it would happen. I've always been content to wander, sew, and do what I can. Just a temporary placement, anyway. What is there to fear?

Hearing all the dragons' voices in my head at the same time is disorienting. Not nearly as fun as I'd hoped. I will update often, but in better light and with more to say. Not that I've ever run out of words.

My old fingers do not care for this quill, nor my eyes for this dim light. They are not old, of course. Just ... tired. I can run with the best of them.

More later.

I am Mari, High Dragonmaster.

Second Month of Spring

Last week, I spent some time with the hatchlings—haven't ever done that. I think they allowed it because they know I'm the High Dragonmaster. See? Privilege has its upsides. The hatchlings are strong, particularly that Luna. Talis was amongst them, actually. Seemed a bit odd, but I didn't question it. He left when I appeared.

Beluas encroach from the south, but I never fear their ugly hides. They'll stay away. If they don't, we'll fight them with the *secundum* of the dragons, which burns hot as the fires of Shalla.

Dragon voices have been ringing through my head for weeks now—I cannot tolerate it anymore. They're constant. Waking me up at night. Screeching if they're close. Whispering if they're far away. How is one supposed to sleep, anyway?

I approached Celeste to ask how she deals with it, for she must. Her account doesn't give enough detail. Breath? Thought? Pah. Before I could even see her house through the trees, I heard her baby. Rumors through the families say her baby isn't satisfied. Bad mam's milk, maybe? Let's just say I remember all eleven of *my* babies, and none of mine were that angry.

I left her to it. I'll figure something out.

A most unusual event occurred just yesterday—a dragon and his rider arguing. Never heard of that before. (Though I've never *heard* a dragon before my appointment.) It was Talis and Sarai, of course. As a normal witch, I wouldn't hear

Talis's part. Today, however, he was in my head. He's calm, in an odd way. A biting, acerbic tone when he wants, which surely angers a firecracker like Sarai. No doubt she wants him to be as outwardly angry and out of control as she is. He's not. I would be. Sarai is vexing.

Talis is beautiful, though—the scales on his belly are bright now that he's on his way out of adolescence.

The hatchling, Luna? She chatters constantly. Follows me on my daily walks, too. Apparently, Talis has been teaching her to hunt. Didn't know he spoke that much with hatchlings, though I have seen him amongst them a second time.

I digress.

High Dragonmaster is a lot more work than I expected. Not that much fun. Although I try to tell Marcus he was saved from a frustrating fate, he rolls his eyes. Let him. He should flatter his elders more. In the meantime, I'll seek out our apothecary while he's still here. Surely Samuel will have some other fix that will aid my troubled sleep.

A potion, perhaps?

I am Mari, High Dragonmaster.

Third Month of Spring

This month brings warmth and banishes the slush. The last of the snow is late to leave, as always. There are places that the sunlight never hits, so we have to wait for the entire world to warm. At least my dresses and socks won't be as stained and wet. That's something. Who has time to scrub?

This is my third month as High Dragonmaster. Celeste's baby continues to bellow at all hours. Psychological issues, I think. That baby needs brewed leto nut milk. Works every time, but no one listens to me.

Samuel finally delivered a sleeping potion last week. Mumbled something about milk of the poppy. Works! Slept like a babe the last few nights. It's done much to restore my humor. Did a jig today. The hatchlings loved it. Someone complained about beluas along the perimeter, but I haven't seen any signs.

In news, my great-grandson, Alfrid, officially finished the circle school. Intense schooling there. It's good. Smart boy. Steady as a whip. Unlike all the other bratty kids here— including the ones I raised—he's never lied. Never spoken a falsehood. Never raised his voice or tried to cheat in school. Steady.

No issues with Sarai and Talis this month because they aren't speaking. Sarai spends too much time with Hubris still. Fine with me. Talis has gone a long stretch without saying a word, even in my head. How a dragon can brood so long, I'll never know.

I fell asleep in the crook of some roots the other day and woke to vines tapping my face. Before I could figure out if I was dreaming, a cry from the village startled me. In the end, the cry for help was nothing, of course. Another complaint about seeing a strange, rippling mirage in the forest. Witches imagining things. I'm starting to wonder if *I* imagined the whole thing. End of a dream, or something? Would a vine tap my face? I confess, I've never spoken with Deasylva. Seemed like a personal experience to me. Months in her service, and I still don't know. I'm not even supposed to be here.

Odd goddess.

It is late, and my elixir moves through my body, calming me. I shall sleep well again. Dear Samuel. I do enjoy him.

I am Mari, High Dragonmaster.

First Month of Summer

The wet heat has descended with no regard for my age and my bones.

I tire of this position. Still, Celeste's child is ill, and Celeste herself is drawn and haggard. Her husband, too, is tired, with rims under his eyes. When I dropped off a loaf of bread for them, I couldn't stand the constant crying, so I left. Something is wrong with that child. Soft bones, maybe. A twisted stomach? Heard of that. Perhaps the poppy elixir would help him too.

Lately, I've taken longer walks to get away from the constant demands of the brood. As I have no dragon that I am bonded with—which makes my appointment even *more* odd—and Perris is still caring for her new hatchlings, I have no dragon to confer responsibility to. Which means that *all* the dragons come to me with the stupidest issues. They sniff something odd. Think they hear something flying overhead. Complain that creatures are transporting around them in the middle of the night without warning. (Is that even possible? Dragonmasters rarely transport because our dragons can't.) I wish myself young again. I'd scale the trees and hide up there. Only hatchlings climb trees.

Received a letter from the High Priestess, but it didn't say much of anything. Had Char pen a reply for me. Dunno what she said.

Several dragons roared in outrage over something between Sarai and Talis. Have no idea what happened—I turned back around and went on a longer walk, then took more of the elixir and slept until the morning. By the time I awoke, all seemed to be well again. If you ask me, *that's* how a High Dragonmaster should lead. Through letting others deal with their own problems. I have enough of my own. You try living in these creaky bones, which are still healthy, thank you very much. Worrying over everyone else? There's no time for that.

I am Mari, High Dragonmaster.

⌇

Second Month of Summer

Last night, I fell asleep in the sunshine, right in the crook of a few tree roots. When I woke up, the wind blew so fast it would have torn my hair free if I hadn't ducked. Branches trembled. Vines whipped around, almost slapping me in the face. Here's the weird thing—only where I was sitting. Everywhere else seemed calm.

Strange, eh?

I stood up to leave and thought I saw a flash of light on the trunk, but these eyes are bleary after a nap. I couldn't be sure. A dragon screamed in my head, demanding help with one of those weird mirages they keep talking about, so I had to leave. Doesn't make sense for *light* to be in a trunk.

Odd forest.

Sarai and Talis helped fight off a belua. Admirably, I must say. Talis has skill with those wings, and Sarai with her bow and arrow. Happiest I've seen Sarai. Talis left immediately after. That night, he slept with the hatchlings but seemed content.

Sarai seems to be taking exception to my long walks, even though I've been on my feet all day helping the brood. Every time I return, she shoves a list of needs in my hand. The walks are only an hour, just to get some peace. Never can do enough around here. Think I'll be easier on the High Dragonmaster after this.

I am Mari, High Dragonmaster.

FIRST MONTH of Fall

Finally, some of the heat has abated.

Not much, but enough to take the edge off. The air changes a bit around fall, you know? Crisper, I suppose. Seems cleaner, to me. Doesn't make any sense, but there you have it.

Celeste left to visit the apothecary where Samuel studied. She hopes it will help the babe put on some weight. Things have been fine without her. Maybe a little easier because Sarai left with her to find a mate amongst Samuel's friends. It's hard to find the right outsider, but my sister found a good one.

Without Sarai, there's no rampant tension between her and Talis, who has positively bloomed in her absence. I heard him talking to Charis and Perris the other day. Conversing. Like a *normal* dragon. He seemed pleasant enough. Sure, he's surly. But he was less ... cagey. Really, whoever allowed Sarai and Talis to merge was lost.

Every dragon has spoken with me directly now. Even Talis approached. He has intense, sharp eyes and a commanding presence. Whether this change can be attributed to turning thirty and coming out of adolescence this summer, or Sarai's absence, I welcome it. Everyone in the brood seems lighter for his jovial spirits. I rue the day Sarai must return.

Someone yelled at me after I returned from my walk because a set of vines nearly swung me off my feet and into the creek. Luckily, these legs can still run. I'll be out of this position soon. I've kept things running and helped control the worst of it. I'll be glad when Celeste takes it over again.

I am Mari, High Dragonmaster.

~

Second Month of Fall

Celeste returns, and so does Sarai.

No husband in tow, at least not yet. Negotiations like these always take time.

A docile baby with fat cheeks and rested parents also returned. Celeste said something about uncommon allergies? At any rate, Celeste is back to her usual spit and vinegar. Speaking of vinegar—the moment Sarai returned, Talis disappeared. Haven't seen him in days. Not even amongst the hatchlings, who whisper about missing him.

Celeste is taking over again tomorrow. After eight months of this, I'm grateful not to have a day more. As of my writing, there are forty-five dragons and thirty-five witches. So many that witches can't breed fast enough to give them all riders— especially when some of us, like me, don't get a dragon. No matter. Many of those dragons are hatchlings or old. We're a strong brood. I'm grateful to contribute.

I leave this book in Celeste's hands. Let her think of my chronicles what she may.

I am Mari, High Dragonmaster.

CHAPTER 4
CELESTE

Second Month of Fall

I am Celeste, High Dragonmaster.

I write only to claim my privilege again. It has been a long eight months, although I see that Mari has chronicled more than her fair share—and on paper that is hard to come by. The night is deep and strange. An odd tingle in the air. I feel an urgency to speak with Deasylva. In fact, I believe I hear vines ...

I will write more later, as of now, I mus—

CHAPTER 5
ALFRID

I am Alfrid, High Dragonmaster.

A massacre has occurred.

I, Alfrid, am now the High Dragonmaster. The eldest, most experienced witch who survived, and I am nineteen years old. Who should bear such a burden so young? There is so little that I know. Even now, my hands shake. There is blood on the paper, but I cannot wipe it off. It has smudged, a testament forever. I must go.

∾

One week *after the Great Massacre*

There is no time to write luxuries now. We have fled the circle of the Ancients and have wandered in Letum Wood for two weeks, I think. No, less. I'm not sure anymore. What we seek most is safety. Thankfully, Talis has taken over. He guides the dragons. I guide the witches. We are walking now. Always walking.

Must go. Fire is dying, and we cannot abide the utter darkness. The same that wrapped us when the massacre ...

I am ...

~

Two MONTHS *later*

We have found our new home, and I am ready to tell my tale.

The place of our new village is a lower, sloping land, at the bottom of two very gradual and gentle hills. A stream cuts through it, providing fresh water. The gentle hill peaks at the top and then flows back down. Talis has begun to mark the territory beyond the crest of the hill. He wants us to hold the higher ground on all sides but to be hidden in the valley.

Tonight was the first time Marta was able to make an actual meal instead of relying on raw wild onions and the rare cluster of leto nuts. Talis has been hunting most of our meat, even though he is exhausted.

The grief of what we have experienced seeps into my soul. An utter delirium that seems to feed off my very bones ... but I am delaying the inevitable now. Let me recount the horrors of the Great Massacre.

Poachers—for that is our closest approximation of *whatever* attacked us—came in the darkest part of the night. The Southern Network has attacked us in the past. I can only imagine they are behind this massacre.

They descended from the treetops and swarmed us from the forest floor. No dragons. Not even that many witches—or so we think. Just magic. Intense magic. Dark magic the likes of which we have never seen. Their greatest weapon was clouds of sparks that billowed like tongues of fire. I cannot describe seeing a wall of sparks moving through your home, devouring witches, consuming dragons in their entirety.

Whoever we fought, we could not see.

The moment I heard Mam's first shriek, I scrambled out of bed. I could hear others screaming near the front porch. All I remember is confusion. Flashes of light. Dragons roaring. Celeste shouting orders. The thick sound of Daid's bare feet against the wooden floor as he ran out of the house. Something fell through the roof with a crash.

I grabbed Milley and Sylvus from their room and shoved them out the back door. We stumbled into the forest and began to run. Chaos reigned everywhere. Dragon fire. Sparks that flew on their own. Some of them landed on my skin and burrowed into my flesh as if they would never stop. They tangled in Milley's hair.

Finally, we slipped into the creek. I dunked both my siblings in the water despite the cool air. The burning stopped, but not the murders behind us. We hunkered into the bracken and watched. Listened. It didn't take long to realize we were losing to whatever was attacking. I only saw shadows.

Then I heard a cry. A scream. I turned to find Marta attempting to cross the stream, but something was following her. An arrow skimmed her shoulder. She stumbled and fell. I ran for her, calling her name. She turned toward me. Darkness followed her, if that makes sense. There is no better explanation I can give. Darkness, like a sheet, soared after her. I pushed her behind me.

Just as I believe I was about to be overpowered, Luna appeared.

She threw her body into the shadow, raking it with her talons. A strangled sound came from the collection of darkness. Otherworldly in its deep, guttural sound. A flash of light, that I later realized had been an arrow filled with silver, cut through the night. Luna dodged it with her deft wings. The darkness retreated after that. Luna motioned us deeper into the forest. I didn't remain to find out what was destroying our world. I simply grabbed Marta, my brother and sister, and darted into the forest after Luna.

Not long after, I heard Talis's roar.

We found him flanked by seven or eight trembling hatchlings. Some threw livid fire. Some cried from injuries or fear. What I didn't know was that he had already hidden many others. He snorted in my direction, and I strode toward him. Other Dragonmaster children flowed to us. I called for them as they came, collecting them. Tea held her nephew, Maximus, Celeste's youngest son, in a bundle in her arms. No doubt they were sent into Letum Wood by their parents.

After an eternity of waiting, I had to accept that no more witches were coming. We plunged into the night to hide.

The screams eventually faded behind us, but I remember the blood rushing past my ears. Talis showed us an underground cave, the entrance barely visible in all the fallen leaves. I pushed Marta and my siblings in first. The rest of the children followed. Talis blocked the entrance with his body, which was nearly invisible in the night. I remained there with him. He attempted to push me inside, but I wouldn't go. I couldn't. He seemed to understand. We stood together, watching. Waiting.

Listening to them die.

All seemed to fall quiet at once. I told Marta to stay with the children. Talis went ahead a little way, scouting it out first. But the poachers—whatever they were—were gone. Talis and I ventured amongst the dead. All lost. All gone. Dragon blood pooled on the ground, scored with marks that make us believe whoever attacked came for the blood. For they attempted to recover even that which had spilled. Horns were hacked off. Talons. Even some heart scales. Celeste was dead atop Perris.

Mam? Daid? Gone. Slaughtered.

The memories begin to blur here. All I remember is the approach of dawn. The strange stillness in the forest. The distant sobs of those left behind. We found two other children—James and Stell—hidden in a closet. I scoured every house. They were the only ones we found alive. The rest were at the cave, taken there by Talis.

Then we left.

We always feared this day, didn't we? Though we rarely spoke of it. It seemed inevitable that a stretch of such peace, in the same place, would end with unexpected fire and death. What could we do? They were unknown witches—if even that—with strange magic, descending without warning. No dragon can fight off arrows filled with liquid silver. How could they obtain such weapons? How could they smelt and painstakingly craft such a terrible design?

Their desperation must have been great, indeed. Desperation or greed. Is there a difference? Some days, I cannot tell.

Talis considers what happened in no such light. Refuses to see any side with compassion. I cannot blame him. My soul aches for all we have lost. Without Talis, what would we have done? We would have all died. The race of forest dragons and Dragonmasters decimated in one fell swoop.

And where is Deasylva?

Aside from her nephew, Marta is the only one of her family who has survived. She mourns deeply. I can feel it in her restless movements when she sleeps by me at night. She and I have already agreed that our handfasting will have to be metaphorical for now. There is much to do. Worrying about a silly thing like a handfasting ceremony feels wrong. We must build new, solid shelters and keep the children and hatchlings alive.

The remaining witches look to me as their leader. I find it

hard to believe that I am. Did this really happen? Is this some strange dream? I feel apart. As if I'm staring down on it all from a distance. But I wake in my own body, saturated in cold sweat, and remember the glassy eyes and the pools of sapphire blood.

Talis beckons. I must go.

I am Alfrid.

~

Four months later

In all, almost seven months have passed.

I don't know what exact day it is, just that we have broached spring. Maybe one day we'll venture out and learn exactly where and when we are. For now, we survive. We're living in hastily constructed tents stretched between tree roots for shelter. When it rains, all are miserable. But at least we're alive.

I could not bring myself to write during the dark, cold winter months. There was much to do between securing a border, hunting, ridding the area of dangers, collecting fire-wood, and helping Talis hunt. Thank the goddess for Talis, who has shown amazing foresight and skill as he scouts areas out. He maintains a cool head when the hatchlings yowl into the night for the mams they will never see again. The sound will haunt my nightmares forever.

All of us are exhausted, the hatchlings most of all. Only Luna has seemingly endless energy. Talis seems to have a special affection for her; she shows none for him. She is less than ten years old and doesn't seem to understand the compliment he pays her. Talis guesses correctly, I believe, when he says that Luna's energy is grief. She hunts squirrels for the hatchlings and somehow manages to keep their spirits up.

After this time of hibernation, I have reconciled myself to our new lives. Our new fate, as Talis would say. As if fate were a merging, shifting thing. As if it were controlled by something other than ourselves. As we emerge back into warmth, I feel I can finally emerge as a leader and face what happened.

I have made a makeshift bedding out of a thin canvas Daid used for the goose ticks we slept on and given it to Marta. Before we left the Ancients, we foraged whatever we could. Linens. Packs. Dishes. Talis speaks of possibly going back by flight, getting more of what we need. But neither of us seem to have the heart to do it. We'll make do with what we can and attempt to store for the winter, as Dragonmasters have always done.

For now, I sleep outside with Talis. There is one witch on guard all night for now. Keeping the fire up. Listening. None of us are ready to trust the dark silence again. The hatchlings all sleep around Talis and myself, which keeps me safe enough to sleep deeply when it is my turn.

I feel I should list the witch survivors. Those with noted last names indicate the three main Dragonmaster lines, which have, by some miracle, survived this disaster. The rest come from slightly mixed lines.

Alfrid Parker, male, age 20
Marta Chandler, female, age 18
Tea Spence, female, age 16
Brig, male, age 14
Chauncey, male, age 12
Stell, female, age 10
Milley Parker, female, age 8 (my sister)
Brock Chandler, male, age 7
James, male, age 7

Sylvus Parker, male age 6 (my brother)
Maximus Spence, age around one year

(You will note that none of these children's parents are listed as survivors. Marta has become the unofficial mother of many children. Tea doesn't speak much lately but has been indispensable in calming the three young boys, particularly at night, and caring for her nephew, who clings to her all the time. Milley is also attached to Marta. She hasn't spoken a word since we left.)

I am Alfrid, High Dragonmaster.

~

Four weeks later

We have named our new home Anguis.

In the language of the ancients, it means safety.

Now that we head into the hot days of summer, life has been easier, though I doubt I will feel it can ever be *easy*. We have built a shelter that the children sleep in. Later, I think it will serve best as a place for all our hunting weapons and pelts, and as a gathering place. For now, until the children have grown and we can build individual houses, it suffices.

Tea insists on sleeping outside with Brig, Chauncey, and I, though I cannot fathom why. She says she prefers the open air. When Maximus cries for her, she soothes him inside then comes back out. What she means about *open air* I cannot fathom. Nothing about Letum Wood is open. As a leader, though, I have learned to choose what battles I face. In this, I let her go. She harms nothing. That leaves Marta inside with the six younger children, who still huddle around her like little chicks when darkness falls. She has stepped into the role of their mother with grace.

Marta, Brig, and the rest of the children have started to

help hunt food for the hatchlings. Luna has proven herself worthy of praise yet again. She not only hunts but has been teaching some of the others to do the same. Squirrels are little more than mere bites to the dragons, but it helps.

Talis and I have already discussed the necessity of a wall to keep us safe. The vegetation is thicker here than it was near the Ancients, but not unmanageable. We plan to build a barrier. More than that, Talis plans to build a reputation. If we offer a strong enough front, no creature will enter here.

Talis has been discouraging the hatchlings from flying. I finally asked him why last night while we moved logs to the boundary wall. Talis wants it to be a wall at least as tall as he is. One day, I have no doubt it will be.

He said to me, *Flying is what brought the poachers here.*

Until he said it, I'd never thought about it. Now I cannot stop. I ask myself constantly why the poachers came, how they knew where we were, and why we had no warning. Perhaps they did observe us flying and returning home.

Sometime after the massacre, I became the High Dragonmaster. I do not know when. But it seems I woke up one day and could hear all the dragons in my head. Which means that there *is* some power that controls this magic. Which supports an argument for Deasylva being real. But if she is, she does not make herself known to me. Celeste spoke of her with great reverence. I see, hear, or feel no goddess here.

Talis snorts fire when I ask about Deasylva. I have stopped asking. Still, I wonder. Should we stop the hatchlings from flying? And if we do, are we depriving them of something that makes them what they are?

These questions, and many more, hang heavy on my mind.

I am Alfrid, High Dragonmaster.

~

One week later

This record is not meant for trivial events, but I find it my only release in this ... unsettling time.

Something approached our camp last night. I could not see it. I heard it gnashing its teeth. Bellowing with a deep, strong voice. It's difficult to explain the fear we felt in the aftermath of the Massacre. Truly, I felt paralyzed all the way to my bones. I armed Brig, Tea, and Chauncey with fire. We surrounded the shelter, where the children cried until Marta managed to silence them with simple incantations.

The creature—or perhaps several creatures—stalked us through the night. I had the impression that it circled our camp, but I can't be sure. We kept the fire burning high. Talis threw fire when it seemed as if it approached more rapidly than usual. It departed with the sun. No footprints or tracks remained in the morning.

A good reminder that a forest like Letum Wood is not our ally and never has been, for it's governed by its own magic and its own rules. A system that we know almost nothing of. If we are to survive, I hope respecting that will be enough.

If it weren't for Talis, all of us would have been killed, I am certain. He sent the danger back with fire and teeth. Although he couldn't destroy it—even *he* couldn't see it, the creature of night—he stayed up all night with us.

Marta believes she is with child, although we have no apothecary to confirm it. Talis is pleased. He says the next generation is the only hope for the race of Dragonmasters and dragons. He promises change and security. So far, he has given it. I cannot say how grateful I am for him.

I agree with him. The hope is in the future.

I am Alfrid, High Dragonmaster.

THREE MONTHS later

Summer has almost passed, I believe. The nights shorten. A new chill sweeps over the trees. It's hard to believe that the brightest part of the year is gone, and many times I still feel swamped in darkness.

Marta is certainly pregnant. She believes she'll deliver in the depths of winter. She says she's not afraid, but I am terrified. I know nothing of childbirth and babies. Tea claims to know a little, but she can't fool me. None of us know what we're doing.

I've been scouting the area beyond the borders of Anguis —before the wall becomes inconveniently high—to see if there are any villages nearby. We desperately need simple ingredients for basic healing potions, some utensils, and new linen for clothes. The children ran their garments ragged this summer. Marta and Tea and Stell have nothing to sew from. Not only that, but I want instructions on childbirth. On complications. On how to prevent Marta from dying. None of us can die. We can afford no losses. Least of all Marta.

We would all fall apart without Marta.

So far, I've seen no village within a few hours' walk. Something that both worries and comforts me. We were a day's ride away from villages at the Ancients and several days' walk. Our isolation was a good thing—and our undoing.

I brought the idea to Talis tonight. He refused.

They must think we are all gone, he said. *Eventually, the High Priestess will send her emissary when she hasn't received the yearly report. They'll see the devastation. Let them assume that the dragons have been killed in their entirety.*

When I asked about the lack of hatchlings, he snorted.

The bodies of the dragons will be gone, he said. *They will only see the blood and the witches. We will be released from the foolish, ancient agreement that binds us to witches.*

There was contempt in his voice when he spoke about the agreement between witches and dragons. Just a hint of it. A flicker. Enough that I did not feel safe asking him further questions, and I left.

Now, I sit alone and stew over Marta and our isolationist state. We cannot subsist on the forest alone. I've attempted to make cloth out of magic or moss or anything else but have had no success. We cannot continue in this way. Not without sewing leaves together and becoming outright heathens. There must be some form of compromise.

I confess, I am afraid to attempt one, and I know not why.

I am Alfrid, High Dragonmaster.

~

Six weeks later

Talis says he hears stirrings of a god, not a goddess.

That Drago, god of dragons, has come. He has usurped Deasylva and taken his rightful place. That the massacre happened because of Deasylva, and Drago has come to provide protection. I'm not sure how I feel about this. The previous *Chronicles of the Dragonmasters* that Daid let me read spoke of Deasylva all the way from the beginning. How could a god take over? Talis spoke of wars between gods and goddesses, and how their fights brought about the Mortal Wars and the forest dragons' eventual enslavement, namely, their duty to protect the castle from Almorran magic. Such a thing seems ludicrous, yet I cannot get it out of my mind.

One cannot argue, however, that if Drago is real, he certainly has taken over to good effect. We have a home.

Safety. The ring around Anguis is built up more every day. Talis continues to provide meat for both hatchlings and witches with this *Drago*'s help. The hatchlings grow strong now. Their memories are sharp, honed. They remember well, and they hold that anger within. They do not fly—except for Luna, whom Talis has a hard time regulating, I think.

Just for now, he says. *Flight will come later, when we are safe. For now, we stay beneath the canopy. We must.*

Everyone else fares well. It seems the scales of our grief have slowly been shedding. The children rarely cry anymore. Brig has proven himself a talented hunter and spends a lot of time with Luna. Maximus is strong and growing stronger. His affection and preference for his aunt Tea is clear. Even Milley is proving to be a good scrounger— she treats the hatchlings with toads often. A precedent I'm not sure we should set. Can't the hatchlings find their own toads?

Brig, Chauncey, and I have managed to build another house. A simple one. Two stories tall, but with an actual fireplace. Thanks to Marta's keen observations—and my experience helping Daid add onto our old house—we have made it as sturdy as possible. The children sleep upstairs. Marta and I have a room downstairs, where she has a proper fireplace. It will be a most welcome addition when the new baby comes, and she desires more privacy. This week, Brig is digging a well, even though the creek isn't far away. It seems we have been able to parse together some semblance of a life here. I admit, I have craved it. Stability.

It seems to have mostly come, which is frightening in itself.

My paper runs short. I have tried again, without success, to request permission to go to a village and get us needed supplies and clothes for winter. Talis refused. The days turn cold. Soon, I may be forced to go against his will in order to provide for us.

If I do, perhaps I'll take Luna. She is feisty and will bear me. Even for a hatchling, she is strong. Independent.

I am Alfrid, High Dragonmaster.

1st month of winter, 1st week, 1st day

I have just returned from the closest village. Much to update.

The cold drove us to desperation—Talis finally had to relent when he realized we couldn't hunt for the hatchlings without proper attire. To say that *this* is the reason he finally consented makes me a little uneasy. Was it our inability to serve the dragons that persuaded him? Or his concern for us?

Surely the latter. Surely.

He finally allowed me to seek out the nearest village—accompanied by Luna, as I requested—and establish means of trading. This was ideal. Talis remained behind to protect everyone else while Luna and I ventured out.

A week passed before we found a destination. It's difficult to keep track of direction in Letum Wood. I confess, I allowed Luna to fly several times, in the deep night and when we were well away from Anguis, in order to help us find a village. The vastness of Letum Wood cannot be contained. Or perhaps my lack of experience with any other part of our Network makes it seem so. At any rate, both of us seemed relieved to be back in the air. Perhaps being High Dragonmaster has some benefits. Luna, at least, is in much better spirits.

Once we saw and heard signs of other villages, I approached carefully. There are at least three villages within a two-day ride of us. We watched the smallest from the treetops for a full day. Butcher shop. Blacksmith. Mercantile. Only a few shops populated the one road that came in and out of town. Many foot tracks poured into it. I believe it's a hub for other witches who live in Letum Wood.

Once I felt assured of our safety, I ventured in, leaving Luna far behind. (I suspect she crept closer—I will never know.) It wasn't long after I stepped into the mercantile that I realized I had nothing to trade or barter with. No *currency*, as they call it. I had only been to a village outside the circle once, when I was ten, with my daid.

Luckily, the owner was kind. I stayed for a week and worked hard for him and others. From the first ray of sun to the last bit of light, I worked. Eventually, I traded for linens, two cast iron skillets, new shoes, an assortment of food that should help us get through the worst of the winter, and even a few sticks of candy.

The villagers were kind; they didn't ask where I was from. I think it's not usual to make inquiries from witches that come here. Foresters, they call each other, and they tend to keep to themselves. My voice was strange to them. Theirs to me. Still, they asked no questions and offered much work. For them, in a world where young, hearty men are hard to come by, there was much to be done. It feels good to know the date again. To have spoken with other people. In what I hope was a subtle way, I was able to speak to some of those with more experience than myself about birthing. Wound care. Toys. Things that I have never thought much of before now.

At least I know we can go back if needed. Talis will not like that I am thinking such a thing, but I cannot help it. I will say nothing of it for now.

I am Alfrid, High Dragonmaster.

~

3RD MONTH OF WINTER, 1st week, 3rd day.

Talis called a council.

A council has not been called by a dragon within my memory; at least, not by a dragon alone. Plenty of Dragonmasters and their dragons called councils together. Everything was together, back then.

The border around Anguis is at least complete, though not tall yet. None of the hatchlings (Luna aside, of course) flew throughout the winter, but luckily food is plentiful. We haven't had a hard time catching food for them, thank Deas —thank whatever powers that be.

The council was a meeting, really. All the hatchlings and witches gathered to discuss the future. We have been here over a year now. For some of us, the horror remains. For some, it ebbs. Or perhaps they just hide it exceptionally well, despite being children.

Talis has been spending much time in thought lately; even I have noticed this. Marta noticed it especially, for she keeps a worried eye on him, lest he push himself too hard. He believes that the Massacre occurred because of three reasons: magic, flight, and Deasylva's lack of care.

For now, he wanted us to promise to limit our magic to that done while flying. Magic, after all, is what descended with those who came to kill us, did it not? Magic, Talis says, killed our family members. Drove us from our home. It's the fault of magic that we're here. He spoke of slowly doing away with old traditions. And, creating new beliefs. New ways of living. Drago, he says, requires more but gives with greater abundance.

I confess that I cannot ... I think ... that is ...

Drago? No magic? Banning flight?

Much of the relationship between dragons and witches stems from the magic we share and the power it gives us.

Shall we kill that piece of our legacy? And what of our bond to Chatham Castle? How can we fulfill the oath if dragons cannot fly, or the Dragonmasters cannot wield our power?

I wanted to point out that Talis wouldn't let us fly, which meant we couldn't do the magic he permitted. But I remained silent because the children were in full agreement. Marta above all else. I see a growing rage in her. Whether it stems from the changes of pregnancy, the fear of living out here when we are mere children ourselves, or just the power of grief that rises in all of us, I cannot be sure. But I can see in her eyes that she loves Talis and will do whatever he says. The children, who have adopted her as mam, follow where she goes. Except for Tea.

Except for me.

My writings must lessen. Not only does Marta eye me with a sidelong glance when she catches me stealing moments with pen and paper, but I fear what Talis would do if he knew I held a relic of the past. While I respect and appreciate all he has saved us from, I do not seek his wrath, which is swift, hot, and sharp as daggers. As High Dragonmaster, I can't imagine he would forgive me holding on to the past. I believe he'd say that I continue to keep a traitorous past alive. But it wasn't.

Not always.

I am Alfrid, High Dragonmaster.

1ST MONTH OF WINTER, 1st week, 1st day

Marta gave birth to a beautiful little boy last winter. We were blessed to have no complications. Talis has requested she bear again soon—I had to explain that it's different for witches than dragon mams. Still, he seems unsatisfied. He believes that our future lies within the women and their ability to bear more Dragonmasters for us to raise.

Ten beluas attempted to attack throughout the last year. Talis and the older hatchlings fought them off. We've been fighting off a hearty bunch of strickenine moss for weeks now. Thanks to the careful maneuvering of the oldest hatchlings and their second fire, I believe we got it all this time.

The wall continues to grow higher and higher around the edge of Anguis. It's a massive space to build up, and the going is often slow. Even though it hasn't yet been two and a half years, the old wood splinters and falls apart. Holes in the wall open. New wood must be found and placed. Talis loves it best when we find massive boulders to reinforce the boundary with.

Between hunting for the hatchlings, creating weapons, stocking up for winter, and attempting to teach the children, time has gone quickly. So quickly. I often feel as if I never see my young son. Marta stays busy with the children. The girls are a blessing. Without them, I can't imagine how we would handle a family of ten, and all of us under the age of twenty-three.

I just returned from another visit to the village. We were able to, with careful attention, make supplies from last year stretch through the fall. This time, I returned more prepared to trade and barter. I had forest lion leather, soft shoes sewn by Marta, and rolled beads that Tea made from dried flower leaves and tree bark. Inventive girl.

Still, I stayed for two weeks and worked. Talis was adamant that if I went, I would listen and pay attention but utter no word of dragons or Dragonmasters living nearby. Once, though, I overheard someone saying that they hadn't seen dragons flying overhead in a while. Another said he thought them gone completely.

I walked away.

Some of my staying was selfish. I craved the time away from Anguis. To hear about the world. To fly with Luna at night for hours at a time. It was risky, but Talis has given no indication that he knows. Luna has doubled in size and determination. Her allegiance to me is complete. I see no affection for anything else in her. Although still chatty, she *has* mellowed. This time, I returned with twice the supplies, which will be a blessing this winter. Marta seems pleased.

In compliance with Talis's desire for safety—the desire of the whole brood, I should say—I haven't done magic in weeks now. I thought it would feel different. My fingers tingle every now and then, and I feel a hollowness deep in my chest, but it doesn't destroy me. It feels like a selfish thing to desire magic and flight when it brought such pain and devastation.

Flight is gone for now. The hatchlings protest allowing witches on their backs after what happened, even after Talis dropped hints of teaching them. I am not pushing any of the witches to merge with the hatchlings once they are out of adolescence.

Without flight or magic, why would we?

Talis still speaks of Drago—often, in fact. Marta has taken to writing down her requests of Drago on small pieces of wood, then burning them. Talis is always very pleased. As High Dragonmaster, I have neither felt nor seen nor heard anything of Deasylva. She eludes me. Perhaps she never was. Perhaps it was Drago all along, and he was tired of being misrepresented.

Perhaps gods and goddesses never existed. For who would allow such atrocities?

I am Alfrid, High Dragonmaster.

～

1ST MONTH OF WINTER, 1st week, 1st day.

This is the last I will see of the true *Chronicles of the Dragonmasters*.

Talis has discovered my secret and commanded me to burn this tome. My allegiance to Talis and his protection is complete. Almost. I cannot go through with it. While change is necessary, erasure is not. This is the only lie I will ever tell—that I obeyed his directions and burned the last memory of the Massacre and our betrayal.

But I will not.

I feel that I must apologize for giving this to Tea for safekeeping, so that I may hide my culpability if Talis questions me. Tea will gladly bear it to a hiding place and ensure someone in our posterity receives it. In fact, she seems eager to do so. If not her, I would give it to Luna, but it is much harder for Luna to mask truth from Talis.

Talis will outlive all of us. So will all the dragon hatchlings. The slippery truth could fade into oblivion. For I can see that those with wounds often allow them to run deep and fester, even at the expense of truth.

Witches and dragons were once equals. Friends. We lived, breathed, and died together, not apart.

I fear this will not be the case in the future.

I must go.

I am Alfrid, High Dragonmaster.

CHAPTER 6
TEA

I am Tea.

Talis has killed Alfrid.

Treachery, Talis said. *Alfrid has betrayed our safety. We cannot abide even a hint of malfeasance.* The brood—and all witches except myself—believes Talis without question. They cannot see that the greatest malfeasance is Talis. Even Marta, who cries silent tears and holds her head high, says nothing to defend her lost husband, who left behind two children and one on the way.

She believes Talis. I can see it in her eyes.

Luna has given me her utter allegiance and vows that Alfrid will not have died in vain. She will not allow Talis to thrive unopposed, even though we must be careful about it. The wrath in her eyes comforts me. Because of Luna, I know I shall be safe, even though some of the children look at me narrowly. They know I felt as Alfrid did about Talis's control.

Alfrid was not treacherous.

The vines assist me in hiding this book, which comes to me whenever I need it. There is no Drago, for I have met Deasylva. She still beats in the deepest heart of Letum Wood.

I am Tea, friend of Alfrid, bearer of the truth, and silent High Dragonmaster.

THE END

THE RONAN SCROLLS

A SNEAK PEEK

A note on the text:

The adventures of Ronan the Traveler first circulated around the reign of the 390th High Priest of the Western Network after the Mortal Wars, about the time that High Priest Isra Mona of the West had been deceased for three centuries.

Ronan's many accounts were copied and distributed in secret for decades. False, incomplete copies abound. I, and many others, have given our lives to protect and expand his truths.

Now, at the sunset of my life, after dedicating myself to the cause of a magic I did not hold myself, I resign these writings to a place of ultimate safety and trust that they will be protected until the world is ready for the truth again.

Here is Ronan's true story.

Signed,

Martorius

~

Durston

3rd day, 4th week, 1st month of spring

Durston, Northern Network

They burned my brother on a stake.

For this reason, my grief and questions have driven me to study his "mental condition," starting in the Northern Network. I feel I must scour Alkarra from top to bottom in my search to understand his life and decisions. My questions cannot be ignored—I feel restless in my heart and soul. He died from this strange ailment—or rather, because of it. His confinement was wrong. He was not crazy. Something was different, yes. But not harmful. Not dangerous.

Something gave him sight. I will figure it out in his name. This seems the best place to start.

Father disapproves. "It is a wild search," he said with a heavy brow. "Rodan was afflicted with madness."

"I don't believe that," I said. "You are an accomplished apothecary, respected through the entirety of the Western Network. You would have seen the signs."

At this, his eyes drooped, as if they ached. Perhaps I could have been softer, but I don't see how. Truth isn't soft. Perhaps my departure makes him feel like he's lost another son. He hasn't been well since Rodan's violent death. He needs the solace that only comes with time. I can see it burning in his eyes, and this yearning for silence is something I understand. Besides, we can hardly meet each other's eyes these days.

Perhaps he knows *my* awful truth.

"I cannot forbid you, Ronan." He passed a weary hand over his face. "You have always made your own decisions— though usually in a laboratory or a library."

To that, I had no rebuttal. His concern is well founded: I am naive in the ways of the world. I have never slept under the stars or hunted for my own food or traveled on my own, despite being twenty-four years old and *only a scholar*.

Still, I go. I must. Redemption isn't free.

With me, I have brought four empty scrolls bound with leather. They curl snugly into a container also wrapped in leather—this ensures they'll be safe in any weather. The container was Rodan's. Two scrolls, the heartiest, will be for my observations; the other two for my scholarly notes, citations, data, and blessed, beautiful, irrefutable facts. These are the things we need the most. It's likely that years will pass before I find the answers I seek.

Was Rodan, my twin, mad? Or did he truly see the future?

Here are the facts on which I base my expedition:

1. My twin brother, Rodan, was burned on a star-shaped stake because he claimed to see the future.

2. His death is my fault.

2nd day, 1st week, 2nd month of spring

Durston, Northern Network

My trip begins without excitement.

I am in the North, a place I never imagined I would go, though I read extensively about it during my geological research several years ago. Already, I miss my island home off the coast.

Durston is where I have procured an inn—I find it to be a charming mountain town. Goats far surpass witches in number. The witches are quite fond of their smelly little flocks. Goats serve several practical purposes here, such as milk, food, and they use the hides as warm winter clothing. Their cheese is delicious on a fried cake, amongst other things.

The views of this wild mountain world are beyond words. Vocabulary fails me when I try to describe the rocky brilliance of these purplish peaks. Landslides occasionally plummet from the top of a peak in a spray of dust, like foam. Distant specks of something in flight lead the locals to make a sign and swear by the mountain dragons.

The locals are kind. They seem unafraid of my questions. When I ask about witches with special abilities, they are unbothered, unlike those at home. They shrug and say little. Perhaps they have not seen many. Some witches watch me from a distance.

Several possibilities occur to me—perhaps these witches are curious, frightened, or don't want me here. Only one of the witches seems intent on studying me, and appears wherever I go. It's a male, with a thick, dark beard and beady eyes. I believe I first incurred his attention at a pub, when I asked the owner about witches afflicted by madness and claiming to see the future.

Perhaps I am paranoid.

For now, I sleep in a makeshift tent on the ground beneath the northern stars. The ground is hard, lumpy, and cold. My stomach already hurts—I wrongly assumed what food I packed would last longer. Exertion truly does sharpen the appetite.

The locals have warned me about mountain dragons, but I'm confident I could be little more than a snack, with my thin arms and meager body—that Rodan used to make fun of constantly. Dragons shall not be a problem.

Tomorrow, I will speak to the local village chief and ascertain what she knows.

3rd day, 1st week, 2nd month of spring

Durston, Northern Network

Mountain dragons accosted me all night, screaming and tearing through the sky overhead. As I write, my hands shake and my teeth chatter—I feel lucky to be alive. The terror of hearing them outside my makeshift tent, as if they would rip me apart, forced me to plunge into the forest and hide. The darkness blinded me as I ran. Bloody lash marks run all over my arms and hands. Sheer luck brought me back to my tent and scrolls.

Eventually, I found a collection of boulders and wedged myself between and underneath some of them. There I remained through the night. My muscles ache—I will have extensive bruising on my left leg and arm—but I am alive.

Daylight is here, and the attacks have ebbed. I shall sleep now and find an inn before evening.

Perhaps this will be more dangerous than I expected.

4th day, 1st week, 2nd month of spring

Durston, Northern Network

The bearded man was in Durston when I went to inquire about an inn. I found no lodging available. He watched me but made no move to come closer.

I spent the entire afternoon attempting to fish. Saw not another soul—which felt good and perhaps kept me from losing all sanity. In the end, after at least six hours of fishing, I caught a small mountain trout. Then I realized I had no idea how to clean the innards. Thankfully, the years Father employed me as an assistant have given me some anatomical knowledge. Still, the fish was hacked to death with a rock that wasn't very sharp.

I had a small meal of poor fish meat and still feel ravenous before sleep. Hopefully, this rocky outcropping, like a cave, will protect me from dragons.

My pride forbids me to return home to Father so soon.

5th day, 1st week, 2nd month of spring

Durston, Northern Network

My attempts to meet the local leader have failed. One

female witch and one male barred my path. They spoke in a language I didn't understand. Despite my fluency in eight languages, I have no knowledge of this one. Managed to scrounge up some greens that tasted bitter, and a young, stale mushroom.

Unseen obstacles appear to be my greatest foe. Only the weather is in my favor.

Later that night

A downpour of rain has left me soaked and chilled to the bone. I write this only that Father may know, if my body is found cold and dead in the morning, that I cared for him.

If you want to read at the rest of Ronan's adventure (as well as get additional information on Watcher and Defender magic!), **visit www.katiecrossbooks.com** to purchase today.

TELL ME MORE

Thanks for finishing CHRONICLES OF THE DRAGONMASTERS!

Can I ask you a favor?

Would you consider dropping a review on my website? I would *love* to know what you thought of this latest adventure.

Please visit www.katiecrossbooks.com and type *Chronicles of the Dragonmasters* into the search bar. When the paperback pops up, you can click on that image.

Right at the top of the page, you'll see a bunch of stars. Click on those (or scroll to the bottom) and tap *write a review*.

Your opinions and review will be 100% safe. Some retailers will actually cull reviews—without explaining why—from readers that have purchased on their website.

That kind of censorship power is a little scary, right?

For that reason, I wanted to provide a safe spot for your thoughts and opinions.

Thank you for considering! The 2-3 minutes it takes you will help other readers know whether or not the book is a good fit for them. Imagine how *amazing* their day will be when they find their next book because of your thoughts.

Thank you so much!

Warmly,

Katie Cross

JOIN OTHER WITCHES

Merry meet!

There is more epic magic and wild places waiting for you.

If you want to stay in-the-know about new releases, get awesome discounts (IE—more books, less money), and have free novels and short stories land in your lap, I've got your back.

Go to www.katiecrossbooks.com to join the other witches on my email list, where you get exclusive, can't-find-anywhere-else kind of stuff.

(In fact, I'll send you some free stories right away—first email!)

Or you can go to The Witchery, which is my Facebook group of other readers just like you. Please visit www.face book.com/groups/thenetworkseries to learn more!

There, you'll see more images of Alkarra, join all your witchy friends, and go to lunch with me on my weekly Coffee With Katie calls.

(No, seriously. I will Uber-Eats you lunch!)

Can't wait to see you there!

—Katie

ALSO BY KATIE CROSS

The Dragonmaster Trilogy

FLAME

Chronicles of the Dragonmasters (short story collection)

FLIGHT

The Ronan Scrolls (novella)

FREEDOM

The Dragonmaster Trilogy Collection

The Network Series

Mildred's Resistance (prequel)

Miss Mabel's School for Girls

Alkarra Awakening

The High Priest's Daughter

War of the Networks

The Network Series Complete Collection

The Isadora Interviews (novella)

Short Stories from Miss Mabel's

Short Stories from the Network Series

Hazel (short story)

The Network Saga Suggested Reading Order

1. The Parting (novella #1)

2. The Lost Magic (full-length novel)

3. The Lamplighter's Daughter (novella #2)

4. Merrick (novella #3)

5. The Rise of the Demigods (full-length novel)

6. Priscilla (novella #4)

7. Viveet (novella #5)

8. Prana (novella #6)

9. Derek (novella #7)

10. The Forgotten Gods (full-length novel)

11. The Returning (novella #8)

12. Regina (novella #9)

13. Leda (novella #10)

14. The Sister (prequel to WOTG #1)

15. The School (prequel to WOTG #2)

16. The Council (prequel to WOTG #3)

17. The Goddess (prequel to WOTG #4)

18. War of the Gods (full-length novel)

19. The Finales (a collection of novellas)

20. Marten (novella #11)

The Historical Collection

The High Priestess

The Swordmaker

The Advocate

The Reader Request Series

The Gods

The Plummet

ABOUT THE AUTHOR

Katie Cross is ALL ABOUT writing epic magic and wild places. Creating new fantasy worlds is her jam.

When she's not hiking or chasing her two littles through the Montana mountains, you can find her curled up reading a book or arguing with her husband over the best kind of sushi.

Visit her at www.katiecrossbooks.com for free short stories, extra savings on all her books (and some you can't buy on the retailers), and so much more.